ADVENTURES IN
URBAN FANTASY

Russ Crossley

53RD STREET PUBLISHING

Dedication

For Rita, for everything you do to make my life better
every day.

Table of Contents

Introduction

I've been writing for a number of years and several of my short stories have appeared in themed anthologies. What I'm presenting here is a collection of five urban fantasies each with it's own unique setting.

Blossom Queen, Barbarian is slightly different in that it starts in an urban setting but then ends up in an alternate universe. The others stay in their urban settings where anything can happen, and usually does when magic or vampires or fairytales are very real. I hope you enjoy this collection of stories as much as I did writing them.

Feel free to contact me on Twitter or Facebook or via my websites listed in my bio. I welcome feedback from fans.

Adventures in Urban Fantasy
Russ Crossley

Published by 53rd Street Publishing

Copyright 2013 Russ Cossley

Cover art: © Amuzica | Dreamstime.com

ISBN 978-1-927621-23-3

Blossom Queen, Barbarian

BLOSSOM LEANED BACK AGAINST the counter beside the cash register with her arms crossed. She watched dispassionately as the gray-haired woman fumbled in her way-too-shiny-to-be-leather handbag for the last couple of pennies. The clear plastic bag containing two onions sat on the belt. The smell of the old cooking onions wrinkled Blossom's nose. The onions were way past their prime, in other words, deeply discounted.

My life as a cashier at Low To You Foods is as exciting as being poked in the eye with a sharp stick.

The line up behind the old woman had grown by ten since she started looking for the two cents.

Blossom considered paying the two cents herself, but this is exactly why these cheap old ladies dug around for exact change.

Skip Lord the stock boy, her friend and wantabe boyfriend, filled her in on customer tactics in the first week on the job.

The old lady stole a glance at her, offered a brief smile, then looked back into the bag and shuffled the stuff inside some more. "I know I had a couple of pennies here somewhere," she mumbled.

Blossom sighed. What's the use? The worst Artie can do is fire me when my till doesn't balance. "It's okay, ma'am. Don't worry about it."

The old lady's wrinkled features broke into a wide grin and she snapped the handbag closed as if it were suddenly on fire.

Blossom bagged the onions in a white plastic bag with the store logo on the outside and handed it to the lady.

"Thank you, dear," said the woman after accepting the offered bag. "I'm going to report you to the manager."

Blossom's pale, freckled brow wrinkled. "Sorry?"

The woman tsk-tsked. "You didn't offer paper or plastic, dear." She turned and walked off muttering about young people today.

Do a person a good deed and they crap all over you.

"I'm with her," said the obese truck driver type after plunking down a six-pack of loss leader beer on the belt.

Unbelievable.

***

Skip leaned against the break room wall, his hands buried in the pockets of his black, hundred percent polyester slacks. Every few seconds he ran one hand over his purple Mohawk, as if to make sure it was still there.

Blossom, supported by her elbows, sat at the veneer lunch table popping her gum as she explained what a rotten day she was having. Finally she finished and lapsed into silence.

"Yeah, bad news, babe," Skip said, in his standard issue dulcet tone. Skip's the Keith Richards of discount supermarkets.

"But sumthin' exciting happened to me today," he said.

Blossom brightened. "Yeah. What?"

"Some guy named Al dropped off a port at the loading dock."

"A port? What's a port?"

Skip shrugged. "I dunno. But it's about the size coffin," he added a little too eagerly. "Wanta check it out with me?"

Blossom studied Skip's emerald green eyes. They were focused on the coffee-stained floor tiles, and he shifted his weight foot to foot. She smiled to herself.

It sounds like this port, whatever it is, is the size of a bed.

After a quick glance at the apple-shaped clock hanging off the grey wall over the Cummings Diesel pin up calendar, she said, "Alright, sure. We have ten minutes."

Skip suppressed a smile, bowed his head then led the way out the back door to the loading dock. The loading dock was empty this time of day. The unionized dockworkers were at the peeler bar for lunch and wouldn't be back until at least two.

The squish of Skip's skate shoes echoed in the quiet as they made their way through the cavernous warehouse between wall-sized stacks of cardboard boxes.

Finally, they rounded a stack of banana boxes and found what had to be the port. Just as Skip described, the thing stood upright and was about the size of an old-fashioned telephone booth.

Cell phones made public telephone booths useless these days. For Blossom and her peers it would be social suicide if they couldn't twitter. Superman aside who needs a booth anymore?_

"What does it do?" Blossom studied the strange device.

She moved closer to peer through the smoked glass door. Only it didn't look like glass. Reaching out she touched the door and realized it was warm, even though the warehouse air was cool.

"I dun' know, B," said Skip. "Do ya wanta go inside?"

Blossom glanced over her shoulder at him, one eyebrow arched. "You want some, huh?"

Skip's cheeks flushed and he avoided her gaze.

I love 'em shy. It's so cute. Guys are easy to manipulate when they're desperate. But what the hey? Skip's cute, and he's fun.

"Sure, bud let's see how it fits."

Skip caught her eye and smiled, his face was the color of the canned beets on aisle six.

Stepping back Blossom looked for a handle or latch that would open the door, but the sides were made of smooth, burnished steel, and the glass was unbroken and smooth. "Hey, how do ya open this thing?"

Skip stepped up beside her and pressed his hand flat on the glass at a point about waist high. There was a click, accompanied by a soft hiss, and the door swung open.

Okaaayyy. A gas attack? Tentatively she sniffed the air. Nope, broccoli and banana. No poison gas.

Blossom stuck her head inside the open door and saw the walls were black unlike any black she had ever seen. It was as if the walls were not there. Strange, but cool.

She stepped inside and Skip followed her close behind. He closed the door behind them.

The darkened interior felt far more spacious than she'd imagined. The only light came through the smoked glass door so they were shrouded in just enough light she could make out Skip's form, but couldn't see his face.

"So, Skip," she paused as her voice reverberated in the cool, mint scented air. "What's next?"

"A trip." His voice was suddenly deeper and strange to her ears.

Without warning her stomach heaved and she felt like she was flying. A bright white light, so fierce it forced her to shut her eyes tight, blinded them.

After what seemed like an eternity, a cold wind made the legs of her jeans flutter and she shivered. Do I smell smoke?

Blinking to clear her vision she slowly opened her eyes to find she now stood next to a cracking fire and rough, damp stonewalls surrounded her. Standing in front of her was a tall, muscular man with his massive arms crossed over his wide chest.

His thick, black beard, streaked with gray, covered his hard features and ran from his square jaw down his front to the middle of his chest. He wore an ornately decorated leather chest plate, matching leather bracelets, wrapped around his wrists, were the circumference of her waist. A large sword, hanging off a belt round his waist, very nearly touched the sandy floor. The scabbard was decorated with ornate patterns reminiscent of spitting snakes and long-legged spiders.

Where am I?

"Father!" Skip rushed to the man who threw his arms wide and encircled Skip's slender form in a bear hug; his weathered features were split by a grin.

After a short embrace Skip turned to face Blossom, his youthful face also split by a wide grin. "This is her, father. The Queen I promised you."

Queen? What is he talkin' about? "Yeah, sure," said Blossom stepping forward she raised one hand to imply an offer to shake. "Blossom Queen at your service,"

The older man smiled wry and grasped her thin arm in fingers the size of sausages. His coal black eyes bore into hers, his cruel mouth formed a grim line. He reeked of smoke and sweat.

She glanced at his hand and suppressed a wince of pain. That's gonna leave a mark.

7

"You seem strong for an underfed girl." The man's husky voice resonated off the stonewalls.

"Black belt, second degree," she said locking her eyes on his and forcing a frown to her forehead.

The man released her arm and his eyebrows arched. "You are a strange one." He walked away, turning his back to her, toward the crackling flames of the fire that was the only illumination in the cave. He shook his head. "I don't know what a black belt is, but I hope my son is right about you."

"Yes, father," said Skip moving closer to the orange, blue and yellow flames. Sparks flew as wet wood caught fire. "Do you not see the resemblance?"

I'm afraid to ask. "Resemblance to whom?"

Skip ignored her and spent the next few minutes making his case. Apparently the late queen was killed in a landslide, she was Skip's mother, and his father was the royal consort and bodyguard. As Skip spoke Blossom she could see growing sadness creep in from the edges of his father's eyes.

She assumed the big guy was consumed with guilt for, not only failing to protect his wife, but also letting his country down.

Hold on a minute, she slapped her forehead with the flat of her hand, what an idiot I am. "Hey, guys."

They ignored her and kept arguing about disposal versus usefulness. A thinly veiled discussion about my future no doubt.

"Guys!" They stopped talking to stare at her. Skips dad's eyes blazed. I don't think rough-and-tumble here is used to a woman speaking her mind.

It's time things changed.

"Listen, I'm sure this is all very nice and dark ages, but I want answers." She crossed her arms and glared at them.

Skips father's cheeks flushed red and he stepped back as he drew his sword from its scabbard in one smooth motion. The long, steel blade gleamed in the glow from the fire.

He silently raised the sword over his head, gripped in both sinewy hands, and charged her. She sidestepped him and he flew past her raging oaths and curses. She planted a well-aimed kick on his bottom. Since he was off balance he fell face first into the dirt with a grunt and a roar of anger.

Leaping to his feet, in a move so quick Blossom thought it impossible for a man his size, he roared and came at her again, his face a snarl, his sword poised to cleave her in two. The look in his eyes told her he would not underestimate her again.

And she knew the longer this continued the more likely she would be sliced up like a birthday cake at a ten year olds birthday party.

Well then, he has to go down quickly doesn't he?

Towering over her he raised the sword in both meaty hands above his head, his sinewy arms rippling in the firelight, his dark eyes blazing. As he leaned into the blow she dropped her shoulder and ran headlong into his abdomen. With a roar of surprise his forward momentum carried him over her to land, with a grunt of surprise and pain, on his back behind her. At the same time he lost his grip on his sword and it fell away to land with a muffled thump on the sandy cave floor just out of his reach.

Blossom spun round then bent over to retrieve the weapon.

She gripped the leather-covered hilt in both hands and, with a grunt, lifted it in triumph. Her fists rested against cross guard and it took all her strength to keep the heavy blade from swaying back and forth. Her arms ached under the weight. Man, is this thing is big. And I thought over loaded grocery bags were heavy.

"Take that, you old goat."

Her adversary snorted like a bull then surprised her by bursting into a roar of laughter. Skip laughed too.

The big man got up, brushed the sand off his arms and chest, and shook grains from his hair. Blossom seeing the sudden change in their demeanor dropped the heavy swords tip to the sand, but kept her grip tight on the hilt just in case they changed their minds.

Blossom glared at Skip. "Skip, what's going on?"

Skip's cheeks reddened. "Huh, sorry, B. My dad sent me to your world to find a new queen and you're her."

"A queen? Me?" Blossom frowned and let go of the sword. It fell to the sand with a <u>thump</u>. Skip's father stood and retrieved the weapon, which he then slipped into scabbard on his belt. "My name's Queen but…" Seeing Skip's father eyeing her, one eyebrow cocked, and his sausage-sized fingers tightening around the hilt of his sword, she decided the rest was need-to-know and he didn't need to know.

Skip smiled. "Yes, you're Queen Blossom and I'm Lord Skip." Skip walked to stand beside his father. "And this is my dad, Greyeagle Mike."

Blossom held out one tentative hand. "Nice ta meet ya, Mike."

Mike frowned at her. "My fault. Sorry." Skip explained," We go by last names first and first names last."

Blossom considered his words. Blossom Queen becomes Queen Blossom? "That's sill —"

11

Mike glared now. Blossom smiled thinly. "That's sooo silky smooth. Just rolls off your tongue, don't you think?"

Mike smiled; revealing a mouth full of yellow teeth, then went to put more wood on the fire from a stack against the cave wall.

I'm sorry I made him smile. "Ok, so now that that's settled, Lord Skip, where am I?"

"About a year ago we found the portal," he began.

Blossom frowned. "Al the port? That's the best you could come up with?"

Skip grinned and moved to sit on a piece of wood set by the fire to use as a bench. She sat on the log beside him. The log was smooth and the fire warm.

"It worked didn't it?" Skip focused on the dancing flames. Picking up a stick he poked at the burning logs sending sparks and flakes of ash into the air.

"Yeah, I guess so but —"

Skip shifted his lean body to face her. "But what? You want to be a cashier at Low To You Foods the rest of your life?"

Blossom grimaced. "No, of course not."

"Then what is it you want to do?"

Blossom picked up a stick and twirled it in her fingers. "I never really thought about it."

Skip's lips formed a wry smile. "How would you like to be the new queen of the Barbarian Horde leading troops into battle against impossible odds?"

Blossom gazed into the flames. What am I doing with my life? Nothing. But a warrior queen, <u>me?</u> She looked at Skip. "What happened to the last queen?"

Skip's eyes turned down at the corner sand his mouth became a tight line. "Accident. She fell off a cliff."

"Fell off a cliff?"

Skip looked away and shook his head. "I don't want to talk about it."

I think I hit his soft spot. "Sorry, Skip. Why don't you tell me about this army I'm supposed to lead against impossible odds?"

***

The sun overhead beat down on them as they marched across the dusty plain. Sparse yellow grass dotted the arid landscape as far as the eye could see. Blossom stopped walking to wipe her brow with the back of her sweat soaked bare arm. The salty perspiration stung her sunburned flesh.

No sunscreen, and no drug stores to buy sunscreen. When they tell you life in the barbarian horde is tough they aren't kidding.

For the tenth time today she shifted the leather breast plate, and grunted as she adjusted the weight of the heavy sword that hung off the belt surrounding her waist.

After a month of intensive physical training wielding swords and maces, and shooting bolts from crossbows, her stamina and physical strength had increased ten fold, but the trek through the desert would test anyone's mettle.

Skip came up beside her. Unlike her, he was breathing normally and his brow was dry as the desert. She had grown fond of Lord Skip. The blue jeans, Nikes and tee's were gone. He looked the part of the warrior prince, with leather chest plate, steel helmet, and sword at his side. And his moves during training were that of a practiced warrior, spinning and expert deflection of attacks from multiple directions. She'd come to learn Skip was far more than a bag boy.

"How much farther?" Blossom accepted the offered water skin from Skip and took a long draw. While the water was lukewarm it went down like mountain spring runoff.

Skip's squinted at the horizon. "Over that next rise I expect we'll see their camp."

The "them" was the Vandals. Lead by a rival monarch, the Vandals were the sworn enemies of the Barbarians. The two tribes had been locked in a titanic struggle for supremacy of this world over the past three centuries.

Glancing over her shoulder at her troops, such as they were, she sighed. A collection one hundred tired bloodied warriors and old men, who could barely stand, never mind fight.

Blossom knew it was a hopeless cause. Her reign would be short but her new life was far better than her life as a cashier at a third string supermarket chain.

Blossom smiled. "Well then, Lord Skip lets you, me and Greyeagle lead these gallant troops into battle."

***

The Barbarian Horde crested the hill to find a sea of tents stretching far into the distance. Flags of red and blue, with a gold and silver crest in the centre, snapped in the dry desert breeze. Horses, camels, mules, tethered to wooden posts pounded into the sand, and scores of wagons with oversized stone wheels brimming with supplies, were gathered along the perimeter of the tent city.

Naturally, armed patrols on horseback spotted them the moment they appeared.

Several of the horsemen immediately began to blow into spiral shaped horns crying out the alarm. The sound was more like that of a wounded animal than musical.

We're going to be the only wounded ones on this battlefield.

Blossom withdrew her sword from its scabbard the blade glinted in the bright sunlight. One charge and we're done, mission accomplished. The Barbarian Horde will be no more, but the queen has fulfilled her duty.

She recalled a speech from Mr. Higgs English class she hoped was Shakespearean. "Into the breach once more, dear friends," she yelled, followed by a war whoop. She then started to run for the line of guards gathering to form a wall of steel and men before the tents. Behind them rows of archers moved up readying their bows.

With a sense of satisfaction she heard behind her the whoops and war cries, and the curses and the cheers, meaning the rag tag army was following her lead.

Breathing hard she raced down the slope toward her destiny. Death could come at any second but she had no regrets. This past month had been the most satisfying time of her life.

"Hold!" cried a woman's voice from the row of enemy soldiers ahead.

Blossom stopped running and lowered the tip her blade to the desert floor. She stooped over and gulped in air. Man, it's too hot and too dry for a run. And my hair is so frizzed I don't think my folicals'll ever recover.

Skip came up beside her. She glanced up at him and saw his concentration was focused on the woman who yelled at them. Raising her head slightly she saw the woman walking toward them flanked by two tall, heavily muscled men in full body armor.

The woman wore an elaborate gold headpiece with wings, and a mask that partially hid her features. Dirty blonde hair, tied in a braided ponytail, lay loose across her left shoulder. Her gold breastplate gleamed in the sun and her suntanned thighs were bare. Leather knee-high boots completed her outfit.

"The Princess," growled Skip.

Princess? Not a queen? What do ya know? I out rank her. "What's her name?" Blossom's voice sounded raspy and dry, she needed water.

Skip, recognizing her discomfort, handed her an animal skin containing water. She felt bad about finishing the last of their water, but if she could talk to the Princess she might be able to save the remaining Barbarian's from certain death.

Skip whispered in her ear. "Her name is Princess Holly."

Blossom straightened and took in the rest of water then tossed the empty animal skin to the desert floor.

Holly Princess? Don't I know her? She shook her head. Naw, can't be. I'm in another universe.

The Princess Holly walked toward them until she stopped a few yards short of them and began to remove her headpiece. Her steady fingers released a strap under her chin then began to pull the helmet off.

Blossom gasped as the princess revealed her face. "Holly? Is that really you?"

"Yes, Blossom." Holly smiled wryly. "It's been a long time."

"No kidding, girl. Benson-Bones-High-School-class-of-'07-long is how long it's been." Blossom erupted in a cry of delight and took a step forward only to be stopped when Skip raised his arm to block her.

"We must fight," he said, his features solemn. "And die," he finished.

Blossom eyed him. "Why?"

He glanced at her as doubt clouded his features. "Huh, I don't know. It's...it's the rules."

Blossom smirked. "Well, I'm changing the rules."

"You can't," blurted Greyeagle Mike who had joined them, his sword in his hand, looking ready for a fight in his armor and feather-adorned burnished steel helmet.

Blossom turned to face Greyeagle and one eyebrow rose. "Who's the Queen, me or you?"

Greyeagle glanced at Skip then back to Blossom. "You are, my Queen."

"That settles it doesn't it?" Not waiting for a response she went to give Holly a hug. The two women hugged for several seconds until finally they stepped back.

"What do you think, Holly? Should we have a talk about our next move?"

Holly's full lips formed a crooked smile as she looked past Blossom at Skip and gave him a quick up and down scan. "Who's the cutey? Boyfriend?"

Blossom laughed. "Yeah, sorta. Can we talk in your tent? I could really use a cold drink outta this hot sun."

Holly tossed her helmet to one of her guards who caught it in his large hands with a nod of his massive head. "Yeah, sure." Her brown eyes narrowed. "This way."

She turned, with her right hand resting on the exposed hilt of her sword, and led the way down the slope to the camp.

Blossom looked at Skip and Greyeagle. "You guys wait here. I'll be right back."

Skip and Greyeagle exchanged worried looks. "Yes, your highness," Skip replied while shifting his gaze in the direction of the retreating Princess Holly.

Blossom shook her head at them then turned away and rushed to catch up with Holly. They worry wayyy too much.

***

After two hours, during which the Vandals troops dispersed and the horse patrols resumed their normal sweep patterns, Holly and Blossom reappeared at the entrance of the largest tent in the tent city. Just behind at to their left trudged a grim faced Skip and Holly's chief advisor a rail-thin, reedy-voiced man called Warkiller Buster.

Greyeagle, standing at the head of the Barbarian Horde, his hands behind him, stopped pacing as soon as they appeared.

Princess Holly's guards formed a horseshoe shape around the two monarchs when they stopped in front Greyeagle.

Blossom began by raising her voice so that it echoed across the camp and could be heard by the expectant barbarians and vandals alike. "Brothers and sisters in arms." She paused to let the words sink in then continued.

"This historic day will go down as the day the Vandals and the Barbarians became true comrades in arms."

Holly continued. "Today I become co-Queen of one united tribe." She draped one arm across Holly's shoulders. "Along with my friend, Queen Blossom we will lead our peoples into a new era."

"And to war against a common enemy," added Blossom, which finally elicited cheers from the soldiers of both tribes. Holly glanced at Blossom and grinned.

Blossom winked. Yeah, sister good thing we were cheerleaders in high school or we'd have been sliced and diced by now.

"Who is this enemy, my Queen?" shouted Greyeagle.

A brief smile curled the corners of Blossom's mouth. "The Legion of Blood."

Greyeagle's brow wrinkled and his eyes narrowed. "I've never heard of them."

"You have heard of the forbidden zone, right?"

Greyeagle nodded.

"While that's where we're going." She swept her across the sky to indicate they and the Vandals were going together.

Greyeagle shrugged. He then turned to face the Barbarian Horde, raising his sword over his head he yelled,

"Victory or death! Our Queen needs us! We will fight along side our brothers the Vandals to destroy the Legion of Blood!"

The horde roared its approval.

He turned back to face Blossom. "Anything else, Highness?"

Blossom grinned at the big man. "Nope, I think that'll do it. Good job."

Greyeagle offered a lopsided grin then left to lead the army down the slope into the Vandals camp to start war preparations.

Skip leaned closer to Blossom's ear and whispered, "Legion of Blood? Isn't that a comic book?"

"Yes," she shrugged, "but it sounds good, don't you think?"

Skip groaned then rushed down the slope to catch up with his father.

With a growing sense of satisfaction Blossom watched as soldiers from the two former enemies loaded wagons with supplies for the long journey ahead. After Holly told her about the forbidden zone it seemed to perfect place for a good old-fashioned war against impossible odds. Throw in a reference to a graphic novel and wa-la you've got a marketers dream.

Blossom and Holly, Queens of the Barbarian Vandals. I like the sound of that, but how am I going to sell it?

Shoeless Moe

THE DAY SHE CALLED ME I sat at my cigarette scarred desk in the dimly lit newsroom with nothing to write about. The city editor had just killed my series about the mob's control of the unions. The editor said they were poorly written pieces. But I knew the real reason was he was getting pressure from the boy's downtown. The mob was throwing a lot of green around these days, and the politico types had become the mob's lap dogs.

She told me her name was Old Woman and that she lost a shoe, a really big shoe. Old Woman claimed she lived in the shoe with so many kids she didn't know what to do.

A fact that would lead to her death, and my arrest for murder.

My name's Rumplestiltskin. I'm a reporter for Big City Bugle newspaper, and my beat is the night desk.

Like every dame in Big City I knew right away she was working an angle. Red headed dames are the trickiest ones. I called up her picture up on the worldwide web as we talked. I saw a woman with hair the color of carrots, so her intentions were immediately clear. And I'm a confirmed blonde man, but redheads and brunettes are okay by me.

From the moment I heard her sweet talk a sour feeling grew deep in my gut. But my weakness for the fairer sex too often gets me in deep.

We agreed to meet on the wrong side of the tracks, out near the Moldy Projects, named after Rusk Moldy, the crooked developer. As it usually does in Big City it was raining hard by the time I got there.

I had the collar of my trench coat pulled up tight around my pointed ears, and shivered when a cold raindrop fell off the brim of my grey felt fedora to run down my neck. That was when I spotted her standing in the yellow light of a street lamp smoking a long cigarette. I licked my lips, and for the millionth time this week, suppressed the urge to bum a smoke. I always pick the lousiest times to give up a perfectly good vice.

Tall and willowy, her makeup heavy, so thick in fact it looked like it had been applied with a pallet knife. Her full lips were painted red, and her pea green eye shadow emphasized her almond shaped eyes.

As I got closer I realized she was much older than she looked from a distance. But then I'm a four hundred year old troll so who am I to call the witches cauldron black?

As I stepped from the thick shadows into the pale light of the street lamp her emerald eyes smiled at the same time as her sensual mouth. Good thing. If I had thought this was a trap I would have used the .38 I kept in the shoulder holster hidden beneath my gray trench coat. The one the cops don't know about.

I hadn't shaved in a coupla days, and my breath probably reeked of the shot of cheap whisky I drank before leaving the office, but hey in my line of work I'm what's referred to as the diamond-in-the-rough.

When Mrs. Woman telephoned she told me her giant shoe had disappeared. When I asked her what she meant by disappeared she explained she'd been on a date with a man and when she came back it wasn't where she left it.

Now in Big City a missing shoe isn't news, unless it's five stories high, and her date is with Milo Grimm, Capo for the Grimm Brothers mob. This dame had gotten my attention.

The Grimm's control the rackets on the west aide. Every speakeasy, gin joint, pimp, and gambling den pays the Grimm's protection money.

Any who refuse disappear into Never Never Land. I've known a few city editors who I often wished would double cross the Grimm's so they'd disappear, but then who'd be stupid enough to cross the Grimm's?

My well-tuned reporter seventh sense told me the dame was gonna make one heck of a story, and I wanted in on the ground floor.

"Hey, doll," I kept my tone light. My let's-be-friends mode was set on charming.

She regarded me coolly as I watched rain drip off the edge of her wide brimmed hat. One perfectly plucked eyebrow arched on her pale forehead. Under her gaze I felt the familiar twinge in that nice-ta-meet-ya place.

"You Rumplestiltskin?" Naturally she already knew who I was, or she wouldn't have been standing under this street lamp. Playing dumb was a way of life in the underbelly of the Big City. Always force the other guy to show his hole card first. She is a clever gal this one.

"Yes, ma'am." I grinned.

Her eyes narrowed and she took a drag on her cigarette, held it for a second or two, then blew the smoke in my face. I blinked and coughed. "Want one?" Evidently she recognized a reformed nicotine addict when she saw one.

"No. Thanks." I wiped the tear from my left eye with the back of one hand.

Her voice was husky with an extra layer of sexy. "So, Mr. Rumplestiltskin, can you help me find my lost shoe?"

"Sure," I nodded, "I know a few people in this town. I'm pretty certain someone'll know who stole a size way-too-big-for-us-normals shoe." I shrugged. "I mean who wants a giant shoe?

Her pencil thin eyebrows shot up. "A woman with too many children, perhaps?" There was an amused edge in her tone.

I nodded and stuffed my hands in the pockets of my trench coat. "Yeah. I know a little about rug rats."

"Really? You don't look like the child-friendly type to me."

I grinned. "I wasn't always a Big City byline ya know." Her sensuous mouth broke into a pleasant smile then she laughed brightly.

How do ya like that? I made a funny, even though I didn't mean to be funny. Now boyo, I cautioned myself, don't let her flattery cause your head to swell to the size of your ego. You're not that funny. I looked around. "So where was this shoe when it went missing?"

She shook her head. "I said it disappeared, remember?"

"Yeah. Sorry. Is there a difference?"

She ignored my question. "Follow me." She wiggled an index finger to beckon me to walk with her out of the protection of the street lamp and into the inky darkness.

When I followed her into the blackness outside the circle of light of the street lamp it was as if I'd suddenly gone blind. I couldn't see even my hand, or anything else, in front of my face. The world disappeared in black ink. She instructed me to look straight ahead and avoid looking back at the light, so my eyes would adjust to the darkness. Old said she wanted me to see something. Something important.

As we stood side-by-side I heard her breathing and smelled her cheesecake-scented perfume. I've never enjoyed sweet desserts, even feminine ones. They rot your teeth and your mind at the same time, and usually they steal your wallet before you wake up in the morning.

After about five minutes of silence, the only sound the pounding of rain off the cracked and oily pavement; my eyesight had adjusted enough so I could make out two abandoned brick walkups. Between them was a large gap. Could this be where the giant shoe once stood?

If it was then this thing had left one colossal footprint. I would hate to meet the owner of a shoe that big.

I frowned. If she lived in one giant sized shoe I wondered where the other half of the pair was.

My answer was a sharp blow to the back of the head and the world disappeared.

* * *

When I woke it was morning. I opened my eyes looking into a face only a bulldog would love. Lieutenant Manny "Mother" Goose of Big City PD's Homicide Division glowered at me from under the brim of his chocolate brown fedora. He gnawed at his unlit cigar that hung from the side of the slash in the middle of his jowly mug; I loosely refer to as a mouth. Mother and I gave up smoking on the same day. It wasn't a good day. I hoped today would be better, but somehow I doubted it.

"Rump, you alive?"

"Unless you're the devil welcoming me to hell, yeah I'm alive." My voice sounded like sandpaper. When his expression didn't change I added, "What happened?"

I groaned when I tried to raise my head and pain shot across my forehead and my guts twisted. I was going to vomit for sure. I eased my head back to the ground and closed my eyes and waited for the nausea to pass.

"Somebody knocked your noodle into next week," said Mother.

My eyes fluttered open and I blinked to clear the fog in my head. "Now I know why you're the detective and I'm the lowly reporter."

As my vision cleared I saw the sky above was gray with billowing, angry clouds, but at least it wasn't raining. Yet.

I managed to raise myself to my elbows as Mother stepped back, his thumbs hooked off the pockets of the vest under his cheap wool suit jacket. He turned his back to me to face the abandoned buildings.

My eyes narrowed as I studied my surroundings. The two abandoned brick walkups were still there, rust-colored bricks covered with black mold. Between them was the largest footprint I'd ever seen. Old Woman clearly wasn't exaggerating. The shoe had to be at least a size four hundred, triple E.

"Where's the dame?" I asked.

Mother glanced over his shoulder at me and nodded to a spot beside me surrounded by banana-yellow caution tape. In the middle of the tape was a puddle of goo. "That's what's left," he said casually.

My eyes went wide and I froze. "What happened?"

"Somebody slimed her," he said simply.

"I can see that, Mother, but who and why?"

"We're not sure why yet, but we suspect it was a lovers spat, or maybe an attempted rape." He paused and swung round to face me.

"You and I've known each other a long time, eh Rump?"

I nodded slowly. I didn't like where he was going with this line of questioning. "Yeah. Sure, Mother you and I go way back. We had some good times and a few giggles."

Mother shrugged and sighed. "Yeah. Good times." His words trailed off. Suddenly his eyes locked on mine. "Listen, Rump I have my orders. People farther up the food chain smell blood. I'm sure you understand."

My mouth twisted in a sardonic grin. "I'm under arrest, right?"

Mother winced like he'd sucked on a lemon and nodded.

I sat up feeling suddenly better. My headache was nearly gone and the knot in my stomach had eased. It all made sense. A for-show arrest, then Mother would vouch for me, and I'd be back at my desk before noon writing the story of the missing giant shoe, the mobster romance gone sour, and the cheesecake scented puddle of goo. What a story this was gonna be.

"I know what you're thinkin', Rump but it's not gonna be that simple," Mother's mouth became a grim line.

I looked at him and frowned. "What do you mean? It's ridiculous to think I'd kill a dame I just met." I walked toward the gap where the giant shoe print was clearly visible in the light brown soil and waved my arm at it to emphasize my point. "I wouldn't kill a woman I hated, never mind some gal I just met. And I only met her because she called me and asked me to meet her here." I scowled at him. Now I was plain old mad. This was the biggest injustice since that idiot baked blackbirds in a pie.

"I think you better hold on, Rump and stop talking. I have to read you your rights so you shouldn't say nothin' without a legal eagle present."

I stared at Mother and realized he was serious. I felt my face grow flush with anger. "You can't be serious about charging me?"

Ignoring me, as if I were a common criminal, Mother pulled back one side of my suit jacket and pulled my .38 from my shoulder holster as he began to recite my rights. "Rumplestiltskin, you have the right…"

I didn't listen to the rest. I knew it by heart anyway. Working the night beat you see a lot of arrests. I could never figure out why criminals always seem to work at night. Especially murderers. What's wrong with murdering someone in the afternoon, or before lunch?

At least then you'd have the rest of the day to do what you want.

But nope, not in Big City. In Big City murders happen after sunset.

I glanced at the goo. She may have been old, but she was a looker. Mother was right about two things; I just met the Old Woman who lived in a shoe, and I was gonna miss her.

I narrowed my eyes to slits. There was something very wrong with all this.

"Do you understand these rights as I have explained them?" finished Mother in the familiar bland monotone he used for all his arrests.

"Yeah, sure. Whatever. But, Mother explain this to me, how do you know this goo is her goo?" I indicated the gelatinous substance behind the yellow tape with a slight nod of my head. I sniffed the air. "And I smell Cinnamon not cheesecake." I felt a growing sense of excitement. I was onto something and my reporter instincts were in high gear.

Mother looked at me as if I'd grown two heads. The cheesecake part is probably a little over the top.

"The lab boys ran some tests," Mother shrugged his wide shoulders. He pulled his handcuffs from the leather holder on his belt and came toward me.

"Put both hands on your head, then place one hand behind your back."

When Mother came up behind me to snap the handcuffs round my wrists I smelled his warm garlic breath then I heard him whisper, "Run."

I had a split second to decide if I should. Naturally, I always follow whispered instructions so I elbowed Mother in the gut. He grunted and I took off running across the gap between the buildings.

I've never been a runner so before I went fifty feet I was breathing hard and sweat poured down my leathery face. My mouth felt like it was crammed full of cotton balls.

I heard a voice behind me that wasn't Mother's yell for me to stop or he'd shoot. I didn't stop and I didn't look back. What I did do was will my rubbery legs to carry me faster and faster.

The distinct sound of a pistol hammer being cocked echoed off the buildings on either side of me. I knew I was seconds away from death by .38 police special. I kept my feet moving, but it was like I was running underwater, because I seemed to be going slower and slower.

I almost made it to the far edge of the buildings, where I'd be able to take cover, when a shot rang out. I tripped and fell face first hard into the mud.

I thought at first I was hit, but there wasn't any pain so I knew he'd missed.

"Rump! Move your butt!" I raised my head and wiped away the mud from my eyes. When I was able to see again I looked back and saw Mother had his gun out and was urging me on with it. I froze when I saw the trial of smoke coming from the barrel and the unmoving uniformed cop lying face down in front of him.

I realized Mother had set me up as a cop killer. Now every cop in Big City would be gunning for me. I wasn't wanted dead or alive I was wanted sooo dead. Et tu, Mother?

* * *

Someone had bought off the locals to make sure I was edited out of the picture. But why kill the girl? And why steal a big shoe? This wasn't making a lot of sense.

I ran up the steps of the brownstone tenement building of the Van Allen Belt working class neighborhood taking two stairs at a time. I was breathing hard as I stood outside apartment 4C.

Along the way here I had stopped in City Park to wash the mud off as best I could in the public restroom.

Three junkies slept peacefully in the stalls when I was running water in the sink. The towel dispenser had stood empty for over twenty years so I was forced to cup water in my palms and scoop it to wash the mud off my clothes and face. The water reeked of rust and decay. Like everything else in this rot infested town the water had even turned on me.

My only hope now was to get out of Big City. And my secretary Cindy Charming was the only hole card left to play. After all she owed me.

I helped her escape the Prince's castle in the bad old days, when the heavy drinking prince had threatened to murder her, and brought her to Big City.

I rapped on the door. The sound echoed down the long hallway. In less than a minute the door opened a crack. The steel chain was visible across the opening. One inquisitive azure eye peered at me.

"Mr. Rumplestiltskin is that you?" Cindy stepped back and the chain rattled against the doorframe then the door swung open. Cindy wore a slip-over-your-head, floor-length powder blue housecoat that accented her honey blonde hair. The housecoat was closed up to her slender neck.

I never had romantic designs on Cindy. She was young when I brought her here and I considered her my little sister.

When we first arrived in Big City I worried her innocence might be corrupted by the dirt and squalor all around us. But she remained the one good person I knew in this town.

I walked in the apartment and closed the door behind me with a thump.

Cindy's apartment matched her personality. A pink throw rug sat under a pine coffee table in front of a pure white sofa. Mustard yellow curtains framed the windows overlooking the street below. A dozen red roses rested in a crystal vase on an end table to the left of the sofa. Their fragrance filled the room.

I looked down at my clothes and hands and realized I better stay right here by the door. There was no way I was going to track mud on her perfect domestic tranquility.

"Mr. Rumplestiltskin what's happened to you?" Cindy left the room momentarily and came back with a towel.

I thanked her and began to dry my face, hands and hair. "We have to get out of town." Her eyes were wide. "Today, Cindy. We have to leave."

She looked at me dumbfounded as if I were speaking a foreign language. "Cindy, if we don't leave today I will die. Do you understand?"

She nodded and her brow furrowed. "Yes, I do but I'm not leaving."

My jaw dropped and I gapped at her. "What are you talking about? Didn't you hear what I said?"

Cindy nodded grimly. "Yes, as I said already I understand but you're on your own. I'm staying." The determination in her tone made me wonder what happened to Cindy Charming, my little sister, and who was this woman standing before me.

"Cindy, what's the matter with you?"

"Nothing. I have a benefactor. He takes care of me."

A benefactor? My gut twisted. Someone had taken advantage of this sweet young girl and corrupted her. 'Who is it?" I asked between gritted teeth.

"Milo Grimm," she said confidently. She crossed her arms over her chest and turned her back on me. "He told me he was going to set you up for a murder rap because he was hurt by the lies you wrote in the newspaper about his business."

I couldn't believe what I was hearing. "But, Cindy Milo Grimm is a mobster, a criminal. He's using you."

She sniffed. "He said you'd say that." Cindy whirled to face me; her normally gentle features were marred by a scowl. "Just because someone's in the bar business everyone assumes they're mobbed up.

"Milo thought about paying you off, but I told him not to. I know you too well. You're a troll with principals." She scoffed. "Principals that'll land you in the gas chamber."

I let out an exasperated grunt like I'd just been punched in the gut. "Cindy, I thought we loved each other."

Someone pounded on the door interrupting us. We looked at each other. "Are you expecting someone else?" She shook her head.

"See who it is and I'll hide in the bathroom." I hurried to the bathroom and closed the door behind me. I climbed into the bathtub and pulled the shower curtain across. Unlike my bathroom that hadn't been cleaned in five months hers smelled of lavender and ivory soap.

I listened intently. I heard her soft tone speaking, not the exact words just a murmur. Then suddenly there were angry words and the thump, thump of pounding feet then the bathroom flew open and thudded against the wall cracking the plaster.

"Rump? It's Mother. You can come out now. It's all over."

I slid the shower curtain aside and saw Mother in his protective vest with his gun in his right hand. He wore a silly grin on his face.

"Did you get him?"

"Yeah," Mother nodded. "Found Milo hiding in a secret passageway in the lady's bedroom." He stuffed his gun back in his shoulder holster then accompanied me to the living room.

Upon entering the room I discovered Cindy and Milo seated side by side on the sofa glaring at the two uniforms standing over them. They weren't going to say anything more, at least not until they met with their lawyer, and probably not even then. We had plenty of Cindy on tape to convict them both for racketeering and conspiracy. It was enough to send them both up the river for long stretches.

I frowned. "Something I don't get, Mother. How do Old Woman and the disappearing giant shoe fit into this?"

Mother laughed. "They don't. We found Old Woman's husband. The shoe is his. When he left town some year's back, he left one shoe behind for good luck. Old woman who has so many children knew exactly what to do, she moved her kids into it."

"So who's her husband?"

Mother grinned. "He plays baseball for the Neverland Giants. They call him Shoeless Moe. His real name is Moe Fofum."

I shook my head and chuckled. "I get it. Moe's a giant."

Mother nodded. "Yup, 'bout as big as they get. His nickname's shoeless because he only wears one shoe when he plays. He came home to retrieve the other one. He told me the kids moved out of the shoe years ago, but his wife loved living in it. A lot more room in a giant shoe that a one bedroom apartment these days."

"You spoke to him?"

Mother nodded. "Yeah. Heck of a nice guy for a giant."

"And I assume Old Woman's not dead," I paused, "but what about the goo?"

He shook his head. "Hair gel. Moe wears the stuff his sponsor gives him. Practically bathes in it."

I chuckled and nodded then glanced at Cindy. She avoided looking at me.

I may never write the story about all this. There is just so much pain and heartbreak one reporter can take after another day on the night beat —

— the night beat in Big City.

The Wizard's Apprentice

ULBERT OF SHAMAN felt the trickle of a collective of sweat beads run down his back beneath his razor pressed white shirt. Fortunately, his father Harmant of Shaman, had bought him a good luck thousand-dollar navy pinstriped suit designed to hide the tell tale signs of his nervous sweat.

The words of his grandmother's rebuke echoed in his mind. "Horses sweat, men perspire, ladies feel the heat," she always told him.

No, granny, this is sweat. Believe me.

After all it wasn't everyday a young apprentice got the opportunity to compete on The Wizards Apprentice reality television show. And of all the reality shows — Demon Survivor Island, Spirits Run Amuck With Me, Love Spells, to name a few of the less successful competitors—The Wizards Apprentice was the big one.

It is the one arena where a young wizard's apprentice got to strut his stuff and, if he won, would lead to the road of fame and fortune.

It was a real road. A road paved with solid gold and lined by diamonds and rubies.

Images of the many professors at Harvard Business School of Magic ran through his head. He recalled the lectures on topics ranging from your standard love spells, or revenge spells, to wizard dress codes, to spells designed to conjure dragons and other undesirable creatures or oddities. To spells that exorcised the ghosts and ghouls haunting the nether regions of tourist castles. To the wealth spells of the corporate elites in their boardrooms where they played with land acquisitions and mergers.

Of course, everything was directed at training him about magic as a business, not the artsy fartsy craft junk that the so-called sophisticated wizards said was the really important magic.

The only thing Ulbert knew for sure was he hadn't gone to magic business school to become a pauper.

Unfortunately, very little of what he had learned in the past six years he had yet to use in practical applications. Until now.

Ulbert was eager, yet at the same time apprehensive, to put his magic training into practical use.

Yup, he'd make the big bucks and then his family would be proud. He'd show 'em.

His fondest memory of his educational experience was at his graduation ceremony where he levitated a five-ton elephant he had conjured up in the air above the stadium to close his valedictorian address. The spell had been perfect, a true demonstration of his magic abilities. It was the principal reason his peers elected him valedictorian. Everyone had been impressed. Not that the spell had anything to do with the magic business but it was certainly a showstopper.

His mentor, Professor Ooth of Sparta, who taught Business and Magic Ethics, and their Impact on Modern Society, had approached him afterwards and reminded him to be mindful of such showy spells. He warned him such magic was only to be used for the advancement of his future employer not to massage his own ego.

'No one will hire a trickster,' cautioned Professor Ooth. 'Magic is reserved for the pursuit of profit.'

Of course, the dear sweet man was quite correct. But then on this television show tricks sometimes made the difference.

The biggest obstacle was getting his ideas through the toughest and most successful wizard of all time.

Merlin of Uther was the one hundred and forty-fifth direct descendant of King Arthur's Merlin. He was a slash and burn corporate magician who used his magic to personally pillage five of the largest international conglomerates in the world. Merlin reputation as a corporate raider of unparalleled tenacity and aggression was legendary.

Even the government regulators were afraid to take him on. Several who'd tried had never been heard from again. It was no wonder Ulbert felt uneasy around the master wizard.

Now he had made it to the final three. And all that was left was the Wizards Battle. It will be the ultimate show down of apprentice wizardry where only wizard left standing will be the victor.

In the dimly studio lighting Ulbert could barely make out the facial expressions of his fellow competitors sitting beside him in a row on one side of the boardroom table. With a slight turn of his head, he shifted one eye to catch a glimpse of their faces.

Shay of Lankister looked nervous; the dark hair on her upper lip was visibly damp with perspiration. She was a solidly built woman, with arms the size of tree trunks, who had once been CEO of Women's Professional Wrestling before being usurped by a more powerful sorceress and losing everything in the process.

Her spell allowed scrawny, string bean customers, who got sand kicked in their faces, to turn instantly into powerhouses of muscle and sinew. During round one, Merlin called her spell work of genius, mainly because after the 30-day trial period the customer would have to pay a million dollars or lose the new them, forever.

Ulbert admired the spell it was a good business idea, but he also knew this Shay's last chance and he wondered where her desperation would lead her in this final round.

The wily Pixie named Prospero sat to the left of Shay farthest from him. Now this magical sprite was a pixie of a different color. He looked like he tipped the scales at over four hundred pounds. Somehow, this loathsome sprite managed to spend his day ingesting one foul smelling cigar after another.

It annoyed Ulbert that Merlin permitted the mountainous imp to puff away on his smelly cigars during filming. Early in the competition, he had thought about complaining, but decided not to take a chance in incurring Merlin's wrath when it became clear Prospero had curried the old man's favor.

Ulbert knew the obese, beady-eyed fairy was his real competition.

The Pixie earned his place at the table by developing a puffy white message cloud that read "POOF", in block letters, every time a wizard made something — animal, vegetable or mineral — appear or disappear.

Ulbert had to agree this innovation was very cool and surprising from a pixie who appeared more gangster than purveyor of the magical arts. Somehow, Ulbert suspected the pixie was getting help from somewhere. Problem was if it was from beyond the mystic barrier then Ulbert really was in trouble.

It was nearly impossible to detect, never mind prevent, interference from the other side. He knew he would just have to be better. Good thing these two looked like they had never set foot inside a good business school, never mind had a degree of any significance.

Ulbert had earned his way to the final table with his innovative Spell-In-A-Bottle. It had been relatively easy to bottle spells since the days of the ancient genies, but his invention had a new twist. When the suck…uh… customer opened the twist cap on the bottle the spell inside would adapt itself to the request most sought after by the customer.

A marketing research study he had conducted in support of his product had clearly shown that what people wanted most was to change their physical body shape. To be beautiful or handsome was more important than money. It seemed instant wealth didn't have as great an appeal as beauty — as if money couldn't buy happiness. Morons.

If people only knew enough to request the ability to become an instant master wizard then everything else would follow soon after.

Ulbert developed the slogan "Twist Your Way to a New You" go with his presentation to Merlin. He thought about twisting his way to winning the competition but he was certain Merlin would quash his spell and he would be eliminated. Merlin's power was absolute and not even a hotshot like him could beat the old man, but one day…watch out old man, here comes Ulbert of Shaman.

The floor director walked up to stand beside Merlin seated in a black leather executive chair his flowing pure white beard combed and trimmed to a neat point resting on the surface of the gleaming black boardroom table.

Ulbert and his fellow competitors sat on the opposite side of the table from the master wizard.

For the sake of the illusion, Merlin wore a flowing royal purple robe and a matching tall, cone shaped purple hat covered in white outlines of stars and planets.

"We're on his two minutes, sir," said the director, a red haired man dressed in blue jeans and yellow open necked golf shirt.

He stepped back out of camera range just as he raised one index finger that meant one minute. After a short pause, which seemed like days, he held up ten fingers then hid them one at a time as a count down. After the last finger disappeared, he pointed at Merlin as the lights affixed to the top of the television cameras to the side and behind Merlin began to glow red.

"Welcome, Ulbert, Shay, and Prospero," said Merlin his brow furrowed and his tone deadly serious. "Tonight one of you will be eliminated while the other two meet in the Wizard's Battle™ to determine who will become the next Wizards Apprentice!"

Ulbert and the others did the obligatory glaring at each other as if they were enemies. The three competitors really didn't much like each other anyway but this was Hollywood and acting the part of the enemy was a requirement for the show. In this case, reality was closer to the truth than many people suspected.

Merlin adjusted his robe by pulling it up his right shoulder with a rustle of fabric.

This well rehearsed signal meant the glaring was to cease and they were to pay attention to the master wizard.

Ulbert shifted his attention to the elder wizard.

The old man's eyes were the color of ice on a cloudy day and they scanned the assembled candidates like radar of the soul. One of these three was going to hold the enviable position of apprentice to the greatest corporate wizard the world had ever known.

Ulbert felt his mouth go dry under the wizard's gaze. Until now, he hadn't thought it possible he would be unnerved or intimidated by the old master.

Merlin cleared his throat then said, "Shay, while your product proposal is truly innovative and impressive I've decided to let you go. Your product isn't one I would be comfortable marketing through any of my companies. While the weight loss business is a multi-billion dollar business I feel your product has little in the way in actual differences from other products already out there. Products like those of my good friend, Martha whose recent weight loss product line is doing brisk sales numbers."

Merlin stood and held out his wand like he was the maestro of the New York Philharmonic. Shay's features visibly paled as her eyes went wide with fear. She stole a glance at Ulbert as if pleading for help.

He watched helplessly.

"Shay, you are fired!" Merlin waved his wand theatrically and Shay disappeared in a puff of white smoke. She didn't have time to utter a word and she was gone.

Ulbert realized he had been holding in his breath and took in a deep gulp of air. Every time Merlin fired someone, he did this. No one had bothered to tell the competitors where they were going, and Ulbert was too afraid to ask.

'Risky business meant taking risks no matter how high,' Professor Ooth had said.

Ulbert stole a glance at Prospero and saw the hideous pixie was leering at him. He calmed himself locked his fingers on the table in front of him and fixed his gaze on the old wizard who was shaking his head in abject sadness at the loss of Shay. No doubt, the audience at home felt the old man's pain. The master wizard was not only a great wizard but it seemed he was also a competent actor.

Merlin's watery eyes finally landed on Ulbert, drifted over briefly Prospero, and then landed once again on Ulbert.

Breathe, Ulbert. Breath.

"And now...to the Wizard's Battle™!"

Merlin dramatically raised his arms over his head as he threw his head back. There was a camera located in the ceiling over his chair so it would capture the dram of his fierce stare. No doubt, the look on his face would give many a child countless sleepless nights.

The floor director appeared beside Merlin. "We're in commercial for six minutes."

Merlin dropped his arms to his sides and rolled his chair back. "I gotta go for a pee. I'll be back as soon as I can."

The director nodded, but I thought I saw him roll his eyes ever so subtly. He kept his head down obviously pretending to be concentrating on the e-clipboard in his pale left hand.

Ulbert stood and stretched his arms and legs. "Quite the deal, eh Pros? You and me buddy." Ulbert grinned at the scowling pixie who remained seated.

Ulbert grinned and shrugged. He casually walked over to stand beside the floor director. "Hey, Charlie, how's it hanging?"

Charlie Redtop looked up from the e-clipboard his expression bland. "You want sumthin, kid?"

"Yeah, as a matter of fact. Maybe you and I can help each other by —"

Redtop's eyes narrowed. "Whoa, kid. Before you go too far I otta tell ya that the chief don't like me bein' bribed. Last guy who tried it is wearing cement overshoes at the bottom of the Potomac."

Ulbert buried his hands in his pantsuit pockets and shrugged. "I wasn't suggesting anything improper… all's fair in magic anv —"

"Shut up, kid. Not another word or you're gonna regret it." Ulbert opened his mouth to speak but Redtop held up one finger to stop him. He shook his head then turned and walked away leaving a red-faced Ulbert standing alone shifting his Italian leather shoes looking like a child who had just been scolded by his mother.

At precisely six minutes Merlin swept back into the room surrounded by the scent of freshly picked mint leaves.

You gotta love that body wash they use in the men's room here, thought Ulbert upon realizing this might be the last time he's able to smell that pleasant odor.

"I thought you said six minutes…and he said…" Ulbert said pointing at Charlie.

"Commercials wait for me. I don't wait for them," said Merlin impatiently. "Take your seat."

Ulbert did as he was told as Charlie counted down the last five seconds then pointed at Merlin.

"Ulbert. Prospero. Here is your final challenge for the Wizard's Battle™." Merlin paused for effect. "Each of you must use your product to steal candy from a baby!" Again the master wizard paused. "The candy must be delivered to this room by the time the show ends and the only rule is; there are no rules."

"How much time do we have?" asked Merlin looking at Charlie standing off camera. Charlie signaled they had less than ten minutes.

Ulbert sat too stunned to utter a word. This was what he spent six years at Harvard learning to do; steal candy from a baby?

He looked over at Prospero who had his eyes squeezed tight and was muttering a spell under his breath.

Ulbert recognized the words and phrases as one of the many languages of the ancients. It was a tongue so old it had been lost to moderns, except to those who studied dead languages. Fortunately, or unfortunately, he had taken Professor Quonset of Queensland's course on dead languages.

Too bad he had slept through most of the old farts boring lectures. His thinking at the time was quite realistic. How would dead languages ever apply to the modern theory of business in a magical environment?

He groaned inwardly. If only…

Wait. Maybe…he rose from his chair, snatched his spell bottle off the table and headed for the elevators. He needed professional help.

Once on the ground floor he saw the large clock with the ornate steel hands affixed to the massive polished brown marble wall across from the bank of fifty elevators. It told him he had six minutes… "Commercials wait for me," he muttered to himself.

He rushed onto the crowded street outside. Looking at the people hurrying by he stopped the first youngish woman he saw and shoved the spell bottle into her hands.

She looked at him her smooth, beautiful features twisted in pure anger. He was momentarily lost for words in the face of such contempt until he regained his composure. "Sorry. I'm a contestant on The Wizard's Apprentice —"

Her expression softened. "Oh…" she looked at the bottle in her hands. "I recognize this. Isn't this that spell bottle thingy…"

"Huh…yes it is. I was wondering if you help me by turning yourself into a baby. Then I will give you some candy and —"

The woman shoved the bottle into his hands and then slapped him hard across his face then disappeared into the crowd.

Tears of pain ran from his eyes and the right side of his face was pins and needles. It took several seconds for his vision to clear. He looked at his Rolex watch. He was two minutes from losing. Not enough time.

His shoulders slumped forward and he headed back to the elevators then back to the studio. He sat down heavily in his chair just as time ran out.

He sighed heavily and waited for the inevitable trip to oblivion.

Nothing happened.

Silence.

He looked over at Prospero's empty chair. Where was the pixie? Stealing a glance at the opposite side of the table, he saw Merlin seated with a wide smile fixed to his wrinkled features. For the first time Ulbert noticed laugh lines at the side of the gray eyes that now looked warm like those of a kindly grandfather.

"Umm…excuse me, sir…what's happening?"

Merlin chuckled and moved his hands off the table to rest in his lap. "This is the part of the show I really love." His eyes had a mischievous look in them.

"You're the winner, son. You beat the odds. You are The Wizard's Apprentice!"

Ulbert sat stunned his eyes wide and his mouth hanging open. "I don't understand…I thought —"

Merlin's laughter echoed off the walls. "Do you really think I would want someone who works for me to steal candy from a baby? What kind of wizard do you think I am?"

A grin spread across Ulbert's face as he thought about the master wizard's words. Yeah. Who would…?

"Where's the Pixie?"

Merlin smirked and looked wistful. "Oh, he's around here somewhere…"

"Credits are rolling," said Charlie Redtop interrupting the banter between the wizard and his new apprentice.

Merlin scowled and dropped his hands to his sides then used them to push himself back from the table.

"Ya know somebody's gotta get someone to invent a new hat." Merlin pulled off his wizard's hat and tossed it to the floor of the studio in disgust. "This thing is hot and uncomfortable —"

"I can, sir," said Ulbert.

Merlin looked disgustedly at Ulbert. "Will someone show this kid the door?"

Merlin rose from his chair and quickly disappeared through a door behind him that Ulbert hadn't seen before.

Ulbert strode purposefully up to Charlie Redtop. "What's going on? I thought —"

Charlie gazed at Ulbert with his droopy eyes and said, in his monotone voice, "You're in Hollywood, kid what'd ya 'xpect?"

End of the Flies

TONIGHT, JUST AS I SAT DOWN to dinner in front of the TV, my wife, Merle, starting screaming and running around the house. Naturally, I ignored her.

This crazed behavior had been happening every couple of days over the past month. I've tried a few times to assure her the sky wasn't falling, but she just wouldn't believe me, so I gave up.

When she ordered me to drop the newspaper I was reading. To help me ignore her, I kept reading. Yes, I ignored her.

Why you ask? She'd done this too many times and it was driving me a little nuts.

Problem is this time I should have paid a little more attention.

This time she was cursed up the yang-yang, and we (meaning all of us) were in real trouble. Fortunately, some of what was upsetting her managed to slip through my husband-filters.

Over the past month she's told me stuff like the government know about a Texas-size meteor about to hit the Earth and wipe us out, but they were withholding the information because we'd all panic. If Texas really was about to land on my head I know I'd certainly be freaked out.

This piece of paranoia crapola came from her hairdresser, an eighteen year old kid who read it on a conspiracy website.

Then there was the inevitable alien invasion. This came from her brother-in-law Albert before they carted him off to a rubber room upstate.

No, Seattle wasn't about to be invaded by little green men, or white sexless beings with big baldheads and eyes proportionally too big for their oval faces (whether they were male or female remains a mystery).

But today there was a new twist. Today she complained some guy, calling himself Mope something (I don't recall the name exactly), walked into the mayor's office demanding the mayor let Mope's people go, or else.

His people? Who has people anymore? These days not even a Wall Street banking executive claims they have people. (And if they do, they keep it on the QT).

And what was this or else stuff? Since my wife is the executive assistant to the mayor she's usually plugged into such things, but she had no idea what this Mope guy was talking about. And, she added, neither did Mayor Billy Ramses.

That was until the curse changed everything.

I flicked the channel changer to the five o'clock early news and turned up the sound. I was sitting with my TV dinner on the aluminum TV tray with the shaky hollow aluminum in front of me, as usual. On the screen the perfectly sprayed and combed channel two news anchor, Peter Hasting, the man with the perfect white teeth, started his newscast in the usual way.

For the past five years he always starts with a flirty joke with the weather girl. But today, for reasons that will become obvious, he suddenly froze in mid-punch line and stared wide eyed into the camera. His face actually changed to the color of wood ash. Not an easy task with all the makeup those guys pack on their kissers.

I've seen him use this particular dramatic tactic many times, to increase the suspense of the story to follow.

I watched all this half-interested in this so-called Big News Development.

"We take you now to Lake Washington where there is breaking news."

"What no tagline? Com'on, Pete, 'ol buddy. Hook me, baby." I spoke at the television, then snorted in disgust, before I stuffed a large forkful of greasy chicken strip into my mouth.

Peter's tone had that deadly earnestness reserved by local news anchors about to report the birth of a new cow to farmer Jones and family. What a maroon.

I glanced at Merle seated to my left in her matching wing chair with her TV dinner on the tray in front of her. She hadn't touched her food. No loss there really, the chair probably tastes better.

I did think it odd that her cheeks were damp with tears and her hands were trembling. I rolled my eyes and turned my attention back to the television in time to see an aerial shot of the lake. It sure looked red. Strange. The sky visible in the background was still as blue as ever.

I chuckled around my mouthful of stringy chicken. "Hey, Merle. Will ya look at that? They broke out the helicopter to report the birth of a calf."

I shook my head then crammed a fork full of the glutinous mash potatoes with the artificial chicken gravy into my mouth. At least I wouldn't have to chew the stuff.

I realized Merle was right not to eat this crap. I grunted and stuck my fork into the rubbery so-called bird meat then shoved the tray away.

A dyed blonde female reporter appeared on the screen standing on the lakeshore. "Thank you, Peter. This is Lori Oldsby reporting from Lake Washington—" I snatched the remote from the end table next to my chair and thumbed the off button. Lori and the crimson colored lake disappeared into blackness.

I got up from the chair, stuffed my hands into the pockets of my tanned Dockers and began to pace back and forth in front of her.

"Ya know, Merle, sometimes I wonder why we stay in this town. I mean we eat TV dinners for supper every night. You work seven days a week for that walking penis of a mayor. And I'm in a dead end job I hate. I mean how long will it be before China takes over the aircraft manufacturing industry. Five years? Ten? Boeing can't last forever ya know. We should move somewhere else."

"I'm cursed," Merle said softly.

I stopped pacing, placed my hands on my hips, and turned to face her. Strange why was her skin green? Maybe she wasn't feeling well.

"Are you okay?"

"I'm cursed," she repeated, only this time her voice had an edgy rasp to it. I must admit it was kinda sexy actually.

"Oh, really? What is it this time? Aliens? The Loch Ness monster? Dracula? Zombies? What?" I snapped my mouth closed. I was shouting.

I crossed my arms over my chest and let out a breath. My frustration with the way she'd been acting for the past month had finally spilled over.

"Sorry." I closed my eyes and whispered, "It's just all this stuff you've been saying lately is driving me a little nuts and—" I opened my eyes and looked at Merle.

Oh crap!

She was brilliant green and a long forked tongue flicked out of her mouth. I don't recall her having a long forked tongue, but it's surprising how a flicking tongue can be a real turn on, even when your wife is turning green.

"Ribit!" she croaked. Her body shape changed before my eyes. She was now sitting on her haunches like a dog. Or a frog…a frog! My wife had become a large frog!

"What's going on here?" I glared at the frog. "What have you done with my wife, hoppy?"

The frog responded with a deep croak again then leapt off the chair leaving behind a pile of Merle's clothes. Now my wife the frog was jumping around our living room naked. What if someone else came into the room right now?

I slapped my forehead with the palm of my hand. What was the matter with me? My wife is a frog, for goodness sake. A frog.

My eyes narrowed. This had to be the work of that Mope guy she talked about earlier. This had to be the or else.

But how do I find him? I certainly wanted my Merle back. And just to be clear Merle the human, not the Merle the frog.

***

After I picked up Merle and put her in the cab of my pickup I drove to city hall. Along the way I passed groups of frogs. They were everywhere. In the designer clothing shops, coffee shops, dry cleaners, hairdressers, jewelry stores, book stores. Everywhere. But the weird thing was there were men frantically trying to catch them. Every time they managed to catch a frog it slipped out of their hands and jumped away.

What was going on? Had the whole world gone frog-centric? Was there a frog convention in town? Now I was being paranoid. When your wife turns into a frog it sure messes you up.

Then it hit me like a foul ball at a Mariners game, there were no women on the streets. Only men and frogs.

Like my Merle, had all the women changed into frogs? But why frogs? Was this Mope guy responsible? Or was it someone or something else? Was it aliens, or swamp gas, or a government experiment gone wrong?

I certainly didn't have any answers. All I had right now were questions. I only hoped her boss; Mayor Ramses would have some the answers.

When I arrived at city hall the guards who were normally at the entrance to the visitor parking lot had disappeared. As I passed the guard shack I noticed two uniforms lying in heaps on the floor, as if the guards had stripped them off and dropped them right there.

I pulled into an empty stall in the lot and turned off the engine.

"Ribit!" Merle croaked at me from the seat beside me.

"Yup, we're here, babe. Don't worry, I'm gonna find a way to make you human again, or my name isn't Rusty T. Quits."

A fly that had been trapped in my truck flew by Merle. Her dark eyes followed the path of the insect then suddenly her long tongue flicked out of her wide mouth and snatched the fly in mid-flight. And just like that the fly disappeared inside her mouth.

"Ribit," she croaked again. She seemed happy to have the bite-sized snack, but I was horrified.

Oh, crap. When she gets normal again how am I going to tell her she ate a fly with her tongue?

I keep a canvas tool bag in the bed of my truck in a locked box. I got out of the cab, with Merle resting on the flat of one hand. I then climbed into the flat bed and unlocked the steel box. I emptied the tools from the bag and carefully placed Merle inside. She didn't protest or try to jump away. I thought about saying, 'Good frog' but it would just sound stupid and condescending to a woman in her condition.

Still her big black eyes gazed at me seemingly trustingly. Before I zipped the bag shut I assured her everything would be fine, though I had serious doubts.

"Hey, pal you talkin' to the frog?" said a man's voice behind me.

I slowly turned around to discover a man with hair the color of snow dressed in all white from his shoes to his suit jacket. The corners of his mouth were curled slightly upward. Was he mocking me?

I hate being mocked.

I scowled uneasily. "Like, yeah. I'm married to the frog so watch what you're saying about her, pal." My day had so far gone so badly I wasn't about to take any crap from anyone, and especially not from a guy who sells garbage bags for a living. Not even if they're good garbage bags.

Now he smiled. "Sorry. No offense meant. It's just that I've met a lot of people today married to frogs, or their girlfriend are frogs, or their best friends are frogs." The smile disappeared. "It's been a strange day."

I nodded then stopped and studied him for a second or two. "Who are you anyway? I've been to city hall many times, and I would remember you."

Both of his white eyebrows rose on his forehead. "Oh, do you work here?"

"No. My wife does." I stuck one hand in the pocket of my Dockers and picked up the tool bag with the other. "Well, she did until...you know." I sighed. "Somehow I don't think they'll keep her on as the executive assistant to Mayor Ramses now that she's a frog."

"Mayor Ramses," blurted the garbage bagman, suddenly excited. "Your wife works, sorry, I mean worked, for the mayor?"

"Huh, yeah, sure...why?"

He came up to me and draped a long arm across my shoulders and began to guide me to the steps leading to the lobby doors.

"My friend, you and I can do each other some good."

"Who are you anyway?" I asked again.

He chuckled. "Teamsters, Local 4402, Sorcerers, Magicians and Spirits Union. I'm the organizer for Moe Sheppard. Jacob's the name. I'm his right hand man. Your wife ever speak of us?"

I shook my head. "No, not really." The guy behind this was named Moe not Mope. What an idiot I am. I had gained new respect for my frog…uhhh, I mean my wife.

But, magicians? Sorcerers? If my Merle ever became human again I'd never doubt any of her crazy conspiracy theories ever.

"So you know this Mope…I mean, Moe guy who threatened the mayor?" I asked hopefully.

We were just outside the twin glass doors to the city hall lobby. We stopped short, too short and I nearly fell forward, but he held me tightly. I'd annoyed him.

The last thing I wanted to do was piss off a magician, or whatever he was. I could be the next one turned into a frog, or something worse like a rat or a pig.

I couldn't imagine spending the rest of my days wallowing in garbage and mud.

Jacob's arms dropped to his sides and he frowned at me. "The teamsters union has no knowledge of any threats real or imagined ever being expressed or implied to anyone."

"Ok, ok, let's not go all Senate-investigation. It's just two good 'ol boys talkin'. I'm only repeating what Merle told me."

Jacob's eyes narrowed. "Who's Merle?"

I rolled my eyes. "My wife. Like I said she's a frog, but I love her, warts and all. She's my frog."

Jacob grinned. "Of course she is. No worries, pal." Somehow I'd become his pal again. "Let's go inside and meet with the mayor and Moe. They're in talks right now."

I studied him. I didn't trust the guy. He seemed a little too slick, like a used car salesman. But then again what did I have to lose? And maybe I could talk this Moe guy into making Merle human again.

I shrugged. "Yeah, ok. Lead on, MacDuff."

He looked at me quizzically, like a dog when it's confused. I'd found his Achilles heel. He didn't comprehend clichés. "It's an expression meaning take me to your leader," I explained.

Jacob shook his head. "Okay, if you say so."

I smiled to myself and followed him through the glass doors into the carpeted lobby. Score one for the janitor.

***

We entered the mayor's office without knocking to find Moe and Billy Ramses silently glaring at each other from opposite sides of his large glass topped desk. There wasn't anything on the desk between them, not even a scrap of paper, never mind the computer monitor I'd seen on Billy's desk the last time I was here. As I recall that was about a month ago, just before started Merle her conspiracy rants. At that moment I could have kicked myself for not believing her.

"Hey, Billy," I greeted the mayor as I set the tool bag on his desk. He glanced at me and nodded without saying anything in return. It was like watching a staring contest, or paint dry.

Billy's jowly features were pasty and his chipmunk cheeks were ruddy. His blood pressure must be about ready to explode.

Moe looked over at me. His arms and face were deeply tanned and his build was reminiscent of an NFL quarterback. Six foot four inches of solid muscle, with a dimple at the end of a wide chin, sure intimidated me.

I've always pictured magicians as gnarled, stoop shouldered old men who wore pointy hats and flowing robes so this guy was a complete surprise.

So much for the Hollywood cliché. I offered to shake his hand by sticking out mine.

Moe smiled at me and stood. He took my hand in his and I was glad when he didn't squeeze too hard. I winced and struggled to not show the pain. The triumphant look in his eyes told me I'd failed. He released my hand and let it drop to my side. The circulation would come back, eventually.

"Hi, Moe Sheppard," he said introducing himself. I couldn't place the accent. Maybe he was Icelandic. I'd never met an Icelandian before.

"Huh, Rusty T. Quits."

"Tquits? Is that French?"

"No, its T period Quits," I explained, "and it's Polish, on my father's side."

He smiled. "So you come from a family of Quitters is that it?"

I was beginning to take a serious dislike to this guy and I'd just met him. "No, we're Quakers actually. We don't believe in violence." I looked him straight in the eyes. "But there have been exceptions."

He smiled smugly.

I wanted to slap him, but since he out weighted my by at least thirty pounds of muscle, I decided to let it go.

"What can I do for you, Quits?" he asked.

"I'd like to talk to, Billy. Privately."

Moe shrugged. "Sure, why not? Mayor Stall-tactic and me have been getting nowhere. Maybe you can talk some sense into him."

Moe and Jacob left us alone saying they were going to the cafeteria to get some lunch. They'd be back in twenty minutes.

Once we were alone I sat in a chair across the desk from a weary Billy Ramses. "Billy, tell me what's going on around here. All the women in town have been turned into frogs." I opened the tool bag and Merle jumped out to land on the desk.

"Ribit," she croaked and blinked repeatedly under the glare of the florescent lights.

"Get that thing off my desk," said Billy raising his voice an octave.

"Billy, this is Merle."

"Oh." He collapsed back into his leather executive chair, a defeated man. He undid the top button of his white dress shirt and loosened his red striped tie.

"They want me to let their people go," he said, bitterly. His eyes were locked on his desk.

"People? What people, and where are they going?"

He looked up at me, his brow creased. "The union wants the city to pay for two weeks in Hawaii every year for all their members. I can't agree to that. The taxpayers would lynch me."

"And who would that be exactly, the frogs, or the husbands of the frogs?"

As if a light bulb had suddenly gone off his features relaxed. "Ya know, I never thought of that." He reached into his suit jacket pocket and pulled out his cell phone. "I should call my wife."

"You mean your frog?"

He stopped his index finger hovering over the numbers on his phone. "Ya know, I never thought of that either."

I wondered how this moron ever got elected. "Billy, what you have to do is agree to their terms and get back your wife and mine and the rest of the taxpayers. It's the only way. Okay?"

"I could nuke 'em," he said.

I shook my head. "No, Billy only the President can order that, and besides who ya gonna nuke, union headquarters?"

"Oh. Ya know—"

"You never thought of that either?" I finished. He nodded sheepishly.

***

A few days later at home in my living room, watching the five o'clock news, with Merle beside me on a new love seat as we watched the five o'clock news snuggled together. (Human Merle that is, not frog Merle).

Peter Hasting was speaking. "Alien space ships have landed in Washington. Preliminary reports are they are demanding we turn over all potatoes…" I reached for the remote and turned him off.

As the screen went dark I looked at Merle. "What do ya think?"

"Anything's possible," she said. I nodded.

Her brow wrinkled. "What is it?" I asked.

"Have you ever had hunger cravings for something weird?"

"You mean like flies?"

"Yeah. Weird, huh?"

I smiled. Yeah, if I hadn't convinced Billy to give in to the union's demands it would have been the end of the flies for sure.

I only hope Moe and Jacob were enjoying Hawaii.

Legacy of the Hunted

I SHIFT THE PREY'S WEIGHT in my arms then lowered it onto its back on the rain-slick blacktop of the trash-strewn, stinking alley. It blacked out quickly after I squeezed its airway closed. I'm careful not to kill it. Not yet. My food is best eaten fresh.

Not that it's heavy. I caught it at an awkward angle when it fell backward is all.

My nose wrinkled under the assault of a putrid mixture of sweat, stale booze, and excrement (not all of it human) wafting around the prey like a cloud of misery. I let it drop the final few inches to land with a wet smack on the pavement. I stand over it and watch the chest rise and fall with each breath.

It'll be better off dead.

Its unkempt gray beard, and shoulder-length white hair reeked of drain cleaner.

Like a lot of the street rats the older ones boil off alcohol in the brand of drain cleaner favored by the addicts. The local merchants stock enough of the killer cleanser to clean the entire city's drains. Damn leeches make money off the misfortune of others.

I shrugged. The cattle's business is none of mine. I feed on them, I don't judge them.

Back in the day my father raised chickens. He never asked the chicken its opinion before he loped of its head.

But sometimes I can't help dwell on who I am, and where I come from. When I do I begin to think like I did in the twenty-first, in the days before I became a vampire. Life as the undead in this century can be challenging. Two hundred years is a long time, and a lot has changed.

There used to be others of my kind hunting these dirty streets. But in the past fifty years I haven't encountered a single bloodsucker. Back in the day I would sometimes join forces with other vamps and we'd herd the prey together as if we were a pack of wolfs. The group hunts ended in thrilling orgies of blood and death. Those days were awesome.

Today the hunt is a loner's profession so I don't think about the old days much anymore.

When I crave rich, fresh blood my memories fade like a morning mist. Not that I've seen a morning in a long time. In fact it's a memory that is badly faded.

Back in the day humans still believed in the supernatural and good and evil. These days the humans worship science instead of God. They don't believe in the undead. They think vampires are a myth from bedtime stories and all I am is a simple serial killer. Perpetuating this myth is my greatest disguise.

I knelt next to my kill, tilted its head back to expose the pale throat, and then sank my fangs into its yielding flesh. The warm, life-giving blood immediately flowed down my throat. I drink until I sense the old one's heart has stopped.

I stand and run my index finger around my mouth to wipe the excess blood off my lips then suck the remnants off my finger as if it's an elixir. I close my eyes and purr my satisfaction from deep in my throat savoring the moment.

Old blood is the best. I estimate the prey's age to be at least forty, maybe even a little older. A good vintage.

My hunting grounds are separated from the cities of the rich and powerful by a twenty-foot high burnished steel wall. The wall is topped with an electrified fence, and automated guard towers at six-foot intervals brimming with deadly firepower.

A single bullet hurts, 300 rounds per second will shred my body into rags. It's difficult to come back form that type of damage.

More than a hundred years ago the poverty stricken and the drug and alcohol abusers were herded to this side of the city and kept here fully expected to die young. Which they usually do with or without my help. As humans are wont to do the poor and disenfranchised breeding habits are reminiscent of the rats that scurry about these dark streets.

As I see it my job is to cull the herd. The rich and powerful need me.

On those occasions when I visit the other side of the wall I witness how the rich and powerful humans live.

Extreme wealth gets you genetic manipulation to create the best bodies money can buy, and rejuvenation technology keeps those fortunate enough to have the price of young-and-beautiful alive for up to two hundred years. There are rumors that they've broken the resurrection barrier. Soon the humans will become immortals.

If this rumor is true it means the Nosferatu are obsolete.

Who wants to be immortal if it means you are an undead hunter of blood when science delivers the same results without the complications of bloodsucking and possible death-by-stake?

It's tough when you're the one born in the wrong century.

Today I sense something's very wrong. A scent reminiscent of an old danger lingers in the air descending on me like a gray death.

I am the last of my kind. When I die there will be no more vampires. I could have made more vampires but why? I don't see any future for my kind.

The eternal struggle between good and evil has been swept aside. A new legacy is about to be born to replace the old ways.

To replace me.

***

I sit upright in the rotting wooden coffin left vacant by the destruction of my vampire master, Rumsfeld.

Over one hundred years ago my master, Albert Rumsfeld, died at the tip of a stake wielded by a vampire hunter calling himself Vengeance.

The hunter moved with inhuman speed to stake my master before he could react.

After a titanic struggle I killed the hunter by impaling him with the very stake he planned to use on me. Though I triumphed I was shocked to discover Vengeance had genetically enhanced super human strength far greater than normal humans.

Since that day I've worried when I will encounter another genetically enhanced super man such as Vengeance. I worry I may not defeat the next one. But I haven't a seen another of his kind since.

"Welcome, my mistress." Peter, my loyal servant, stepped from the shadows into the fading daylight across the cracked and stained cement floor. The retreating sun casts a chaotic pattern of jagged light formed by the remains of the glass in the broken basement window.

Peter is my most recent blood-slave. He's blond and young, no more than nineteen, with thick, muscular arms and legs. He's dressed in the rags common on this side of the wall. His addiction to designer heroin is forgotten under the influence of my deft touch. After I bit him our blood mingled. Now he hovers between life and death ready to do my bidding. I've made him a better man by saving him from the curse of addiction.

"Any word from Alicia?" Climbing out of the coffin I stand barefoot on the rough cement floor. A thin smile passes over Peter's lips. He nods.

"Be ready to brief me in a few minutes." Dismissing him with a wave of a hand I watch him shuffle into the deep shadow until he sits again on his stool. I smile inwardly.

I love a having a blood-slave. It's so cool being powerful.

As is my practice I do my daily stretches in the nude. The early evening air is thick and heavy with humidity, but I don't sweat. Not that my ageless, undead body needs exercise but I've been doing morning stretches since I was fifteen years old and I'll be damned if I'm stopping now.

When I finish I run my hands through my curly, ink-black hair to smooth the more unruly hairs and move to a scarred wooden chair where I threw my clothes before going to sleep.

Alicia Dickson is my spy on the other side of the wall. Her mission is to scout for the threats I know are coming, and to alert me to impending danger. I took extreme risks to obtain fresh clothing for Alicia.

Alicia is the daughter of the Director of city security, who has a soft spot for his only daughter that somehow recovered from her syntho-heroin addiction. She is the perfect mole, and the perfect slave.

I quickly dress in my black leather pants and matching top until at last I pull on the flat soled leather boots that rise half way up my calf's. The leather is cool against my skin.

"Peter. Tell me the news."

Peter rises and walks to stand in front of me, his hands folded in front of him, his handsome features placid. In another life we could have been lovers, but such human-centric urges have long ago vanished from my consciousness.

Peter turns, reaches down and retrieves a white cardboard box tied with string sitting on the floor next to his stool. It reminds me of a cake box.

"What is it?"

"A gift from Alicia's father." Peter's voice trembles ever so slightly. Without my enhanced senses I never would have noticed Peter is upset and my internal warning bells are going off.

He hands me the box. I hold it by the string, which I use to carry it to my coffin. I close the lid with my free hand and set the box on top of the polished oak casket. I break the string and slowly open it. What's inside the box is not a cake.

Inside is Alicia's dismembered head.

***

I slip into the shadows in the alley just as a surveillance droid appears from a doorway. There are a lot of droids on the street tonight far more than is the norm. They're hunting for something. I hope it isn't me but deep inside I know exactly what they're seeking. A vampire named Lilly Ames. Me.

A pair of gunmetal gray droids appeared at the other end of the alley floating above the brick roadway on their antigravity streams. Suddenly the alley becomes as bright as high noon. I cover my eyes until they adjust to the sudden intrusion of light. Normal light doesn't harm me.

Good thing they're not using infrared lights.

Of course the humans don't believe in vampires anymore. It wouldn't occur to them to install special lights just for me. They think I'm a serial killer. A mentally defective human on a killing spree.

I blink to clear my vision and wait for the droids to act but they stay frozen sweeping the alley with light. It's as if they're waiting for something, or someone.

"Madam," says a shrouded figure, that steps between the two hovering droids. His eyes are hidden in the shadow created by his wide brimmed hat. I know this humans a man because the voice is deep and thick. This human has strength and confidence.

A twinge in my gut signals me to be cautious. My nostrils twitch. This man smells of danger. He is what's been bothering my senses

His square jaw is covered with dark stubble and he wears a western style duster right out of the old west. I see he even wears black leather cowboy boots. Finally he tips his head back to reveal obsidian eyes that scowl at me from beneath the brim of his well-worn hat.

The guys a cliché right out of the twenty-first century vampire movies.

Is he kidding?

I immediately scold myself. I have to be cautious and control my impulse to rush at him.

I let the left side of my mouth curl upward and my eyes narrow. I brace my legs and prepare for the attack I'm certain is coming. My acute hearing detects the movement of air behind me and I realize two droids have taken up positions behind me to prevent my escape. Not that this will work.

"What do you want, hunter?" I say in a low growl. My fangs extend.

The hunter takes two steps forward and swings aside the right side of his coat to reveal a holster with the butt of a pistol showing.

"You think bullets will kill me?"

I'm surprised when he shakes his head.

"No, of course not." A slow smile spreads across his chiseled features.

It dawns on me this man knows what I am. My gut tightens. His gun has to be loaded with silver bullets. As if reading my thoughts he sweeps aside the other side of his coat to reveal a row of four wooden stakes in leather loops hanging from his belt.

"Coming from a costume party?" I say, my voice leaden in my ears.

He shakes his head again this time slowly his dark eyes never leaving mine. "No. I'm a vampire hunter."

I snort. "Vampires? Who believes in such fairytales?"

"More like nightmares, actually." With inhuman speed he snatches a stake from its holster and hurls it at me in one smooth motion. It cuts the air with a swish racing for the center of my chest.

The distance separating us is no more than fifty yards so the wooden missile covers the distance quickly. Without my enhanced reflexes I would already be dead, but with a flex of my legs I spring upward to the rooftop of one of the buildings bracketing the alley. One of the droids immediately captures me in a bath of light. I stand on the edge of the roof gazing down at the hunter looking up at me.

He doesn't look surprised. This worries me.

"Nice move." He chuckles and crosses his arms. "Thank you, Lilly, you've just confirmed what I told him."

I cock a single eyebrow. "Confirms what to whom?"

The hunter removes his hat and bows. He stands straight as his generous mouth forms a wide smile. "Let me introduce myself, Lilly. My name is Malice. You were acquainted with my late brother." His eyes narrow. "Until you killed him, of course."

I stare at him and slowly I begin to realize who he is. I recognize that face, but it's impossible. He's dead. I killed him a hundred years ago.

***

I pace the basement stopping occasionally to stare at the pile of bones lying in one corner of the room. The rotting wooden stake still sticks out from between the age-brittle rib cage. The flesh had long ago rotted away and the rats had scattered the small bones from the extremities like the feet and the hands to who knows where. The upper torso, hip and leg bones, and the skull are the only larger bones still intact. But the real point is he's dead.

I killed him.

I stopped pacing and slapped the flat of my hand repeatedly against my right leg and folded my bottom lip repeatedly. It's like I'm ten again.

Is Malice a twin? I shake my head.

No. My senses say otherwise.

He's real. They must have resurrected Vengeance to come after me. But why give him a new name?

And he knows my name. How?

I turn to glare at Peter sitting quietly on his stool his features placid as always. I recall Alicia's sightless blue eyes staring up at me from within the box. The dry brown blood pooled around the severed neck. Her death came suddenly. A very sharp blade was used to remove her head. The style of her execution bothered me. A story told to me by my master came to me. I stroke my chin with my long fingers and try to recall Albert's tale.

Albert loved to tell stories about his days as a member of the undead. He'd been a vampire for six hundred years before he made me. I was the atypical innocent, blushing bride, nineteen, on her honeymoon with her new husband, Kelly.

I smile grimly at the memory of that day then walked to the window to stare at the sliver of moon visible through the shattered window. I remember that night better than any other.

Without warning Albert came out of the shadows and sunk his fangs into Kelly's neck.

I recall being frozen with fear watching the life in Kelly's pale green eyes slowly fade as he died. His last breath left him his eyes rolled up to reveal the whites, then he collapsed like a puppet with its strings cut.

I willed my legs to move but I couldn't move, a scream caught in my throat. Unable to speak, unable to move, unable to scream, Albert came at me his eyes red as if a reflection of the fires of hell.

I felt his cold breath on my neck, then the searing pain of his fangs as they pierced my vein. I recall the blackness creeping in from the edges of my vision and my body becoming weak. Albert's strong arms held me up as I sank into a black abyss. I remember wondering how such an old man could be so strong. Finally I passed out.

When I woke I found myself in this basement propped in a corner. I raised my head and saw Albert seated on a stool his arms crossed over his sunken chest. His flesh was white a bone and his clothes looked old fashioned, yet still new.

His red-rimmed eyes stared at me. Then he stood over me with his arms still crossed. "How do you feel?"

I blinked and moved first my legs then my arms. "Surprisingly good."

He chuckled dryly. "You, my dear are now one of us."

Albert explained that he was a vampire and rather than killing me he made me a vampire. I would live forever and never age.

Now for a narcissistic gal of the twenty-first century this sounded pretty good. When I asked about Kelly, Albert seemed truly sorry he'd been unable to save my new husband. To this day I think he was lying.

At first I resented Albert but he was my master so I let it slide. Over the next hundred years I learned all there is to know from him about my life as a vampire. In my own way I grew to love him.

The story that twigged my memory involves a nineteenth century vampire hunter named Barnabas Sloan.

Sloan's weapon of choice was a saber he used to sever a vampires head. Besides wooden stakes or silver bullets through the heart, removing a vampire's head does the job nicely. The trick is the head must be buried separately from the rest of the body ensuing the vampire would not rise.

In some traditions the vampire's headless corpse would be burned to ashes.

Did Barnabas Sloan kill Alicia?

If the common link to recent events is Sloan then I have a chance. His deathblow is to use the sword. This is a close in weapon.

I've lived for two hundred years and a master vampire has instructed me. I have the advantage.

But I'm worried. If it is Sloan then he sent Alicia's head as a message. I eye Peter and it dawns on me his earlier nervousness is out of character. He has information I need.

My hands drop to my side and my hands ball into fists.

***

Before Peter dies he tells me everything.

Alicia's father commissioned a research project to resurrect a nineteenth century vampire hunter and, worse, to clone him after the public saw an image of me killing a prey. They doctored the image to make it appear I killed a rich citizen when in fact my kill was a homeless drug addict on this side of the wall.

Her father seeks revenge after he discovered Alicia was my blood slave. And they found a way to chemically nullify my blood slaves and turn them against me. I broke Peter's neck after he told me that.

Vengeance was the result of an early experiment to clone a vampire hunter. The clone was enhanced with super steroids making him strong and aggressive.

The disappearance of Vengeance resulted in the project being shut down.

Eighty years later a new series of cloning experiments resulted in an army that over the past fifty years hunted and destroyed the vampires, all except me.

Of course the big game changer is the elite have finally achieved immortality. They no longer need me.

Worse yet they successfully resurrected Barnabas Sloan and made several clones designed specifically to hunt for me. One is called Malice.

A thump from the room above startled me. I glanced at the window and quickly realized I had no more than an hour until sunrise. I need a new hiding place.

Peter must have been implanted with a homing device. Malice is upstairs and he knows I'm here.

My hunch is confirmed when I hear the soft pad of his boots starting down the stairs and the hum of a droid guarding the top of the staircase.

My body tenses as I wait for the basement door to open. The footsteps stop on the other side of the door.

"Lilly, don't attack. I need to speak with you." It's Malice alright.

"Why should I trust you?" I call back.

"Because Alicia told me about you."

At the mention of Alicia's name I decided to let him enter. There is something in his tone that I trusted, something I'd sensed earlier in the alley.

He didn't lie, or maybe he was a poor liar. Whatever it was for the first time in two hundred years I decided to give a human a chance. Before I kill him.

"Come," I said simply.

The door creaked as it opened and Malice stepped into the room. He wore a lopsided grin on his narrow features and his eyes sparkled with amusement. He was dressed as before in the costume of a nineteenth century hunter.

"Lilly. It's so good to see you again."

I crossed my arms over my chest and glared at him. "Say what you came to say."

His grin dissipated and he sweeps his hat off his head in one smooth motion releasing a nest of brown curls that fall around his face. He moved to my casket and placed the hat on the lid.

"I've come to you with a proposal." His soft brown eyes locked with mine.

"Oh, and what might that be?"

He swept the right side of his duster aside and slipped his thumb over the heavy leather belt. His pistol's absent.

He must have noticed my look of surprise because a brief smile passed over his lips. "As you can see I'm not armed."

I considered killing him immediately but for reasons I cannot explain I hesitated. This proposal he spoke of intrigued me. "Go on."

"Barnabas proposes you work for us."

I cocked one eyebrow. "Work for you?"

"Yes, as a vampire of course."

I dropped my arms to my sides, chuckled grimly then moved closer to within easy striking distance. I didn't see the usual fear in his eyes just before I sink my fangs into humans. This man had no fear.

"Before you kill me I must tell you the immortals want you dead. They've hired Barnabas and I to do it."

"But in a few seconds you'll be dead then all that's left is Barnabas." I emitted a deep growl. Malice didn't move and his eyes remained placid.

I sighed and took a step back. "Alright, so what do want of me?"

"You and I and Barnabas must form a syndicate. Without each other we are all dead. None of us is meant to be alive in this century. We are an infection to them. The immortals plan to eradicate this infection beginning with you, then us, and then they will eradicate all humans considered imperfect." He draws out this last word.

I realize immediately what he's telling me. Without a vampire to hunt two clones of a nineteenth century vampire hunter would become redundant. They needed me to exist and I needed them to exist. We are co-dependant. He's right.

"So, what's the plan?"

***

I have an apartment in the city now, and I have a job.

I kill for hire, for food and for self-preservation. Barnabas and Malice control the city through terror and assassination with me as their instrument of death.

The first human I killed for Barnabas was Alicia's father. I enjoyed that one. I cared about Alicia. Her father deserved to die.

I even have a new blood-slave, an immortal named Randy. He'll be with me forever.

The legacy of the hunted has shifted from me to my prey. The immortals make an excellent food supply. For the first time in a long time I'm looking forward to the next two hundred years.

About the Author

International selling author, Russ Crossley writes romance under the name R.G. Hart, mystery/suspense under the name R.G. Crossley, and science fiction and fantasy under his own. This year there will be re-issues the romantic comedies, Bachelorette: Zombie Edition by Champagne Books, and Antique Virgin by 53rd Street Publishing, paranormal romantic comedy, Zomopolis, and a new western romance entitled, The Fire In Their Hearts co-authored with R.S. Meger will be published in 2013 by Champagne Books. Also, look for another Aloha adventure, Bloody Betty Queen of the Pirates coming in the spring of 2013 from Champagne Books.

In addition the near future suspense novel, The Last Serial Killer by R.G. Crossley was recently released by 53rd Street Publishing in ebook and trade paperback versions.

He has sold several short stories that have appeared in anthologies from Pocket Books, St. Martins Press, at Smashwords, Amazon, and other e-retail sites.

With his wife, romance author R.S. Meger, he owns and operates a small press publishing company, 53rd Street Publishing.

The company began in April 2011 and now has over one hundred e-book titles and a number of print titles, with more planned in 2012 and 2013.

He is a member of SF Canada and the Greater Vancouver Chapter of Romance Writers of America. He is also an alumni of the Oregon Coast Professional Fiction Writers Master Class taught by award winning author/editors, Kristine Katherine Rusch and Dean Wesley Smith.

To find a complete listing of his work check out his website http://www.rghart.com, http://russstory.blogspot.com.Razor's blog can be found at http://razorandedge.blogspot.com

Feel free to contact him on Facebook or Twitter. He loves to hear from readers

Other books by the Author

Titles as R.G. Crossley

Short Stories

Razor and Edge Mysteries
The Kidnapping of Billy Buttons
String of Pearls
Death by Clown
Beggin' For Murder
Ragged Ice
The Grand Central Mystery
A Strange Case of Undead Murder

Jazz Stiletto Mysteries
A Day Without Sunshine
Skullduggery

Non-Series Mysteries
Mirror Image
Dangerous Waters
Cape Disappointment
Boomerang
The Watcher of Wayburn Street
The Apprentice
Drip!
A Beautiful Friendship and The Parrot of Doom
Robine's Diary
The Christmas Club

Loose Ends
Splatter Pattern
It Takes Two

Anthologies
The Adventures of Razor and Edge:
Five Tales From The Quirky Detective Team

Novels
A Bad Case of Loyalty
The Last Serial Killer
Shear Murder

Titles as Russ Crossley

Novels
Attack of the Lushites
Revenge of the Lushites (coming soon)

Short Stories
Countdown
Shoeless Moe
Round Up At The Burger Bar:
The Story of Trixie Pug, Parts 1, 2, 3, 4, 5, 6, 7
Five Minutes
Blossom Queen, Barbarian
The Secret
The Family Line
End of the Flies
With Death You Get the Eggroll
The Penguin Sleeps With The Fishes
Only The Worthy

Hero For A Day
End of Empire
Strange Bedfellows
Big Business
A Perfect Crime
The Wise Guy and The Pirates
In Search of the Perfect Cup
T.I.N. Men
The Legend of G and the Dragonettes
The Incredible Mr. Fix-It
Lock Stock and Barrel
Divided Loyalties
Cave of Wonders
A Family Empire
Until We Meet Again
Dragon Rising

Presents Anthology Series
Five Tales of Urban Fantasy
Five Tales of Bizarre Detectives
Tales of Mystery and Suspense
Five Tales of Weird Fantasy
Spies, Detectives, & Heroes
Tales of Twisted Crime
Tales of The Unexpected
Tales From Space
10 by Russ Crossley
Round Up At The Burger Bar: The Story of Trixie Pug,
Parts 1- 5 The Beginning
Worlds of Science Fiction and Fantasy
More Tales of Mystery and Suspense
Ladies of the Jolly Roger

Justice Served

Titles as R.G. Hart

Short Stories
Tikka's Big Day
"My Partner the Zombie" —
Hungry For Your Love Anthology
(St. Martin's Press)
Big Hairy Deal
One Red Shoe
A Bad Day in Lunden Texas
Hook Island
Grind Manor
Bloody Betty, Queen of the Pirates (coming soon from Champagne Books)

Novels
Bachelorette: Zombie Edition
(from Champagne Books)
Antique Virgin
The Fire In Their Hearts
with R.S. Meger (coming soon from Champagne Books)
Zomopolis